A GOLDEN BOOK • NEW YORK

DC
COMICS™

Copyright © 2016 DC Comics.
DC SUPER FRIENDS and all related characters and elements
are trademarks of and © DC Comics.
WB SHIELD: ™ & © Warner Bros. Entertainment Inc.
(s16)

RHUS36847

The stories contained in this collection were originally published separately by Golden Books
as follows: *Bad Weather!* in 2015, *Flower Power!* in 2014, and *Super-Pets!* in 2015.

randomhousekids.com

ISBN 978-1-101-94023-5

MANUFACTURED IN CHINA

10 9 8 7 6 5 4 3 2 1

Random House Children's Books supports the First Amendment and celebrates the right to read.

By Frank Berrios
Illustrated by Ethen Beavers

Gotham City's baseball team was in the middle of a game when suddenly, cold, rock-hard hail crashed down on the field!

"Don't worry, I've got the bases covered!"
Green Lantern said. With his power ring, he
formed a giant umbrella over the field.
"Thanks for the save!" replied a coach.
"That storm just came out of nowhere!"

Meanwhile, in Gotham Harbor, Aquaman was battling a fierce storm.

"That ship is out of control!" he said. Using his power to talk to sea creatures, Aquaman asked some whales to tow the ship to shore.

Nearby, Hawkman scooped up a boat.
"Looks like you could use a lift!" he said.

Not far away, ice crept over the city's biggest bridge. Superman realized it was going to break in two! The Man of Steel used his heat vision to repair the damage. "Yay, Superman!" the people cheered.

At that same moment, The Flash was using his super-speed to save two children caught in a dangerous lightning storm.

"Hold on tight!" said The Flash as he dodged the deadly bolts.

At a nearby work site, Batman and Robin had their hands full dealing with a flash flood.

"These storms can't be natural," Batman said. "As soon as these workers are safe, we'll need to find out who's behind all this bad weather."

Back at the ball field, Green Arrow spotted a couple of ice-cold criminals! "Leaving the game so soon?" he asked as he released two arrows.

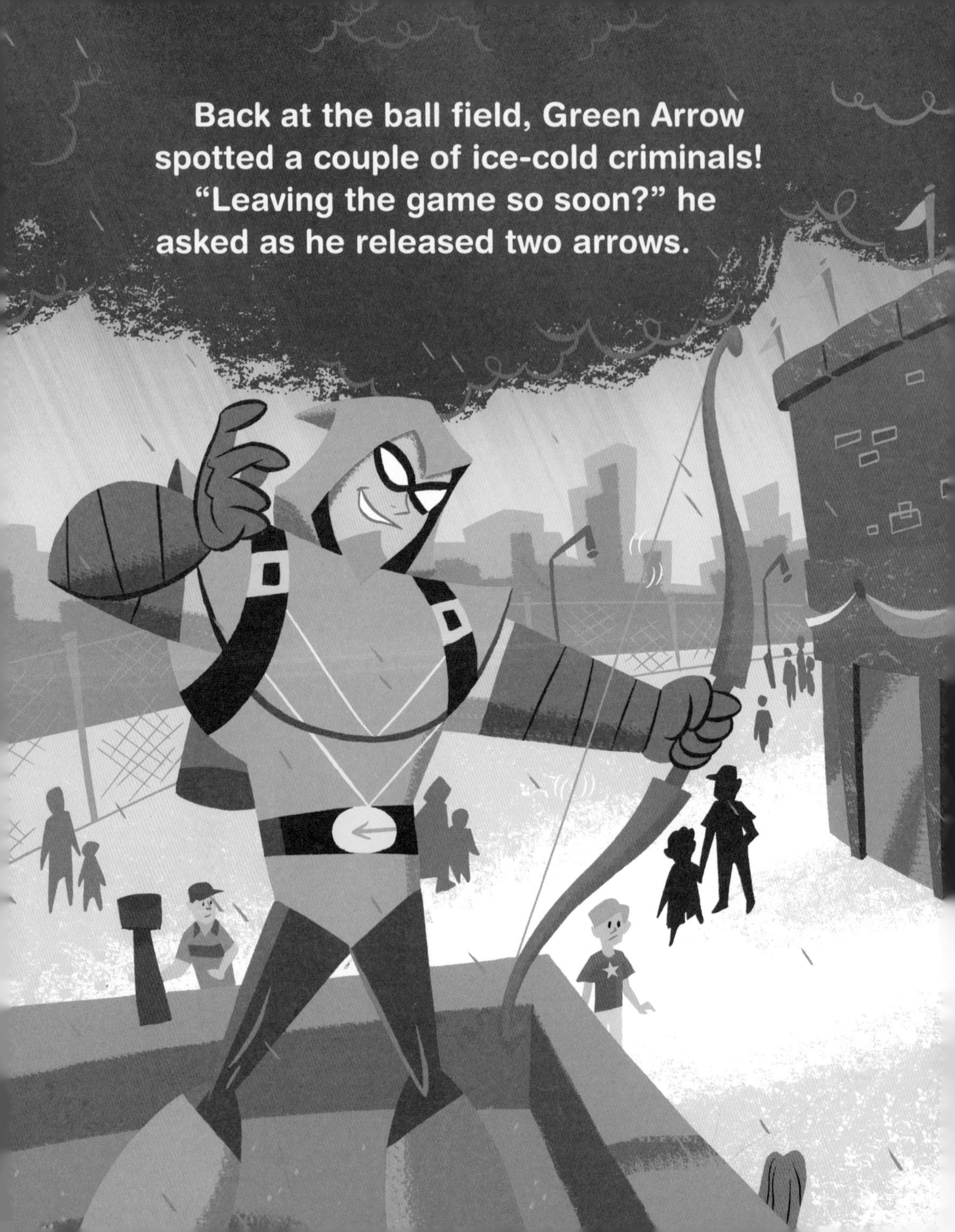

The arrows tripped up the thieves
and pinned the stolen cash to the wall.

In his hideout, Mr. Freeze looked over his stolen loot.

"Your backpack weather machine worked like a charm," said one crook. "The Super Friends were so busy with the storms, we took whatever we wanted!"

"What about the money from the baseball game?" asked Mr. Freeze. The thugs didn't know.

"No matter," replied Mr. Freeze. "We now have enough to create a weather machine that can freeze the whole world!"

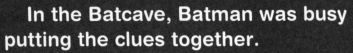

In the Batcave, Batman was busy putting the clues together.

"There has to be a connection between all of this strange weather," said Batman. "And I've found it! The storms have hit every inch of Gotham City—except for the zoo!"

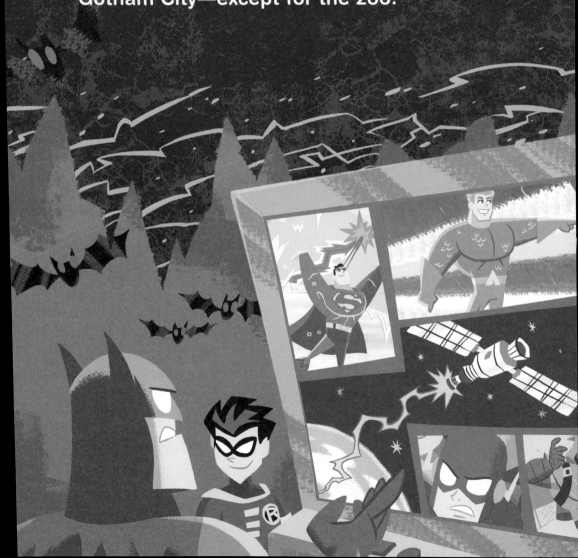

Batman radioed Superman. "I've found a satellite that is sending powerful energy waves toward Gotham City. I need you and Green Lantern to check it out while the rest of the Super Friends take a trip to the zoo."

When Superman and Green Lantern found the satellite, it whirred to life—and attacked them!

"They've found the satellite, which increases the effects of my weather machine!" Mr. Freeze shouted. "We can't let them find us, too. Time to make our escape!"

The villain and his crew quickly packed his Ice Sled with all the stolen loot.

Mr. Freeze blasted out of his hideout just as Hawkman arrived on the scene.

"Do not try to escape!" ordered Hawkman. Then, without warning, he was hit with a freeze ray! The winged warrior was trapped in a block of ice—and falling fast!

EMPEROR PENGUIN

Suddenly, Green Arrow leapt from the shadows! He launched a safety-net arrow, saving Hawkman seconds before he hit the ground.

The Flash raced in just as Mr. Freeze
unleashed a whirling tornado!
   "Foolish Flash!" shouted Freeze. "Did you
think catching me would be so easy?"

When the other heroes arrived, Mr. Freeze used his weather machine to shoot icicles at the Dynamic Duo. Then he created hurricane-force winds to hold Superman and Green Lantern back.

"With the weather at my command, nothing can stop me—not even the Super Friends!" bragged the icy villain.

"Time to team up!" said Batman.
"Robin, let's take out those treads!"
    "Good job," said Superman. "Now
I'll use my heat vision to melt that
freeze cannon!"

"And I'll deliver the knockout punch," added Green Lantern. "Bull's-eye!"

"Ooof!" Mr. Freeze fell backward, smashing his backpack weather machine. As the machine fizzled out, so did the wild weather!

"Sorry to rain on your parade," Green Arrow told Mr. Freeze. "But neither snow nor heat nor ice will keep the Super Friends from delivering bad guys like you to justice!"

DC SUPER FRIENDS ™

Flower Power!

By Courtney Carbone
Illustrated by Dan Schoening

It was a sunny afternoon in Gotham City. Wonder Woman and Batgirl were on patrol when a blazing light streaked across the sky!

BOOM! The glowing-hot object crashed into the nearby botanical garden.

"Let's check it out!" called Wonder Woman.

"I'm glad you're here," the head gardener said. "As soon as that meteorite landed, the plants started doing really strange things. . . ."

Wonder Woman noticed that the plants seemed to be growing quickly and moving on their own. A tendril shot out and wrapped around her arm!

WHOOSH! A dark figure swung in on a jungle vine, snatching up the glowing meteorite.

"Poison Ivy!" Batgirl gasped.

"I could sense this space rock's plant powers from miles away," the villain declared. "It's just what I need to start my plant army!"

"Poison Ivy is using the meteorite to control the mutating plants!" yelled Wonder Woman. The tentacle-like tendrils squeezed the two heroes tighter and tighter.

Batgirl reached into her Utility Belt.
She grabbed her Batarang and cut
through the slithering vines.

The heroes chased Poison Ivy into the desert greenhouse.

"You two need to get the **point**—nothing can stop me now!" the villain cried.

Poison Ivy aimed the meteorite at a cluster of cactus plants. Fsst! Fsst! Fsst! Suddenly, the cacti started firing sharp thorns at the heroes!

Jumping forward with lightning speed, Wonder Woman used her silver bracelets to deflect the thorns. **Zing! Zing! Zing!**
"**Sharp** thinking!" said Batgirl.

Wonder Woman and Batgirl dashed after
Poison Ivy into the outdoor gardens.
"Time for my a-MAZE-ing escape!"
Poison Ivy exclaimed. She ducked into a
large hedge maze ahead of the heroes.

Wonder Woman and Batgirl chased Poison Ivy through the twists and turns of the maze. But Poison Ivy was using the meteorite to make the greenery lash out at the heroes!

Branches swatted them angrily, and grass tugged at their heels. Wonder Woman spun her magic lasso, mowing through the branches, while Batgirl hacked at the plants with her Batarang.

Wonder Woman and Batgirl found the villain near a row of bushes trimmed into the shapes of animals.

Wonder Woman told Poison Ivy, "You're a bad seed . . ."

". . . and we're about to nip your plans in the bud."

"I'll teach you once and for all not to meddle with me," Poison Ivy warned. She held the meteorite above her head. Rays of sunlight made it glow with alien power.

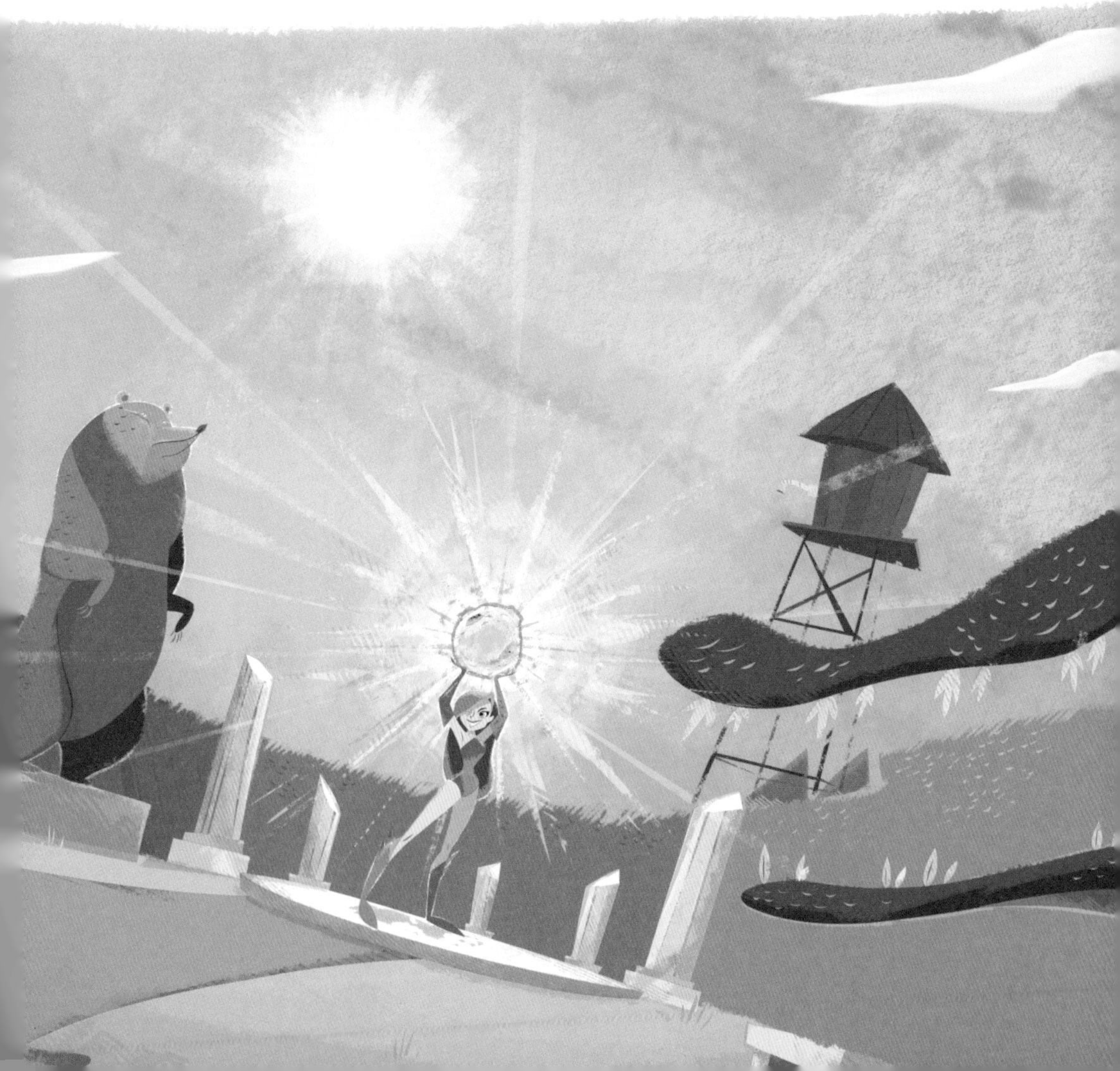

The flowers and animal-shaped shrubs uprooted and began creeping toward the heroes!

"We're surrounded!" Wonder Woman shouted as she and Batgirl prepared to defend themselves.

"I think it's time the whole world went **green**, don't you?" Poison Ivy cackled.

Batgirl had an idea. She threw a
Batarang at the meteorite in Poison Ivy's
hands, shattering the space rock.

Wonder Woman used her magic lasso to snare a pipe on the garden's water tower. She pulled—and water rushed out, soaking Poison Ivy!

Poison Ivy began to grow flowers and leaves. Her roots dug into the ground.
"Nooo!" Poison Ivy cried. But it was too late. She was turning into a plant!

"Your plans are all wet," Batgirl told Poison Ivy.

"At least she picked a great place to put down roots," Wonder Woman added.

"It looks like you have a new Ivy exhibit," Batgirl told the head gardener.

The gardener laughed, thanking the heroes.

"We're always glad to help **weed** out trouble!" Wonder Woman said.

SUPER-PETS!

By Billy Wrecks
Illustrated by Ethen Beavers

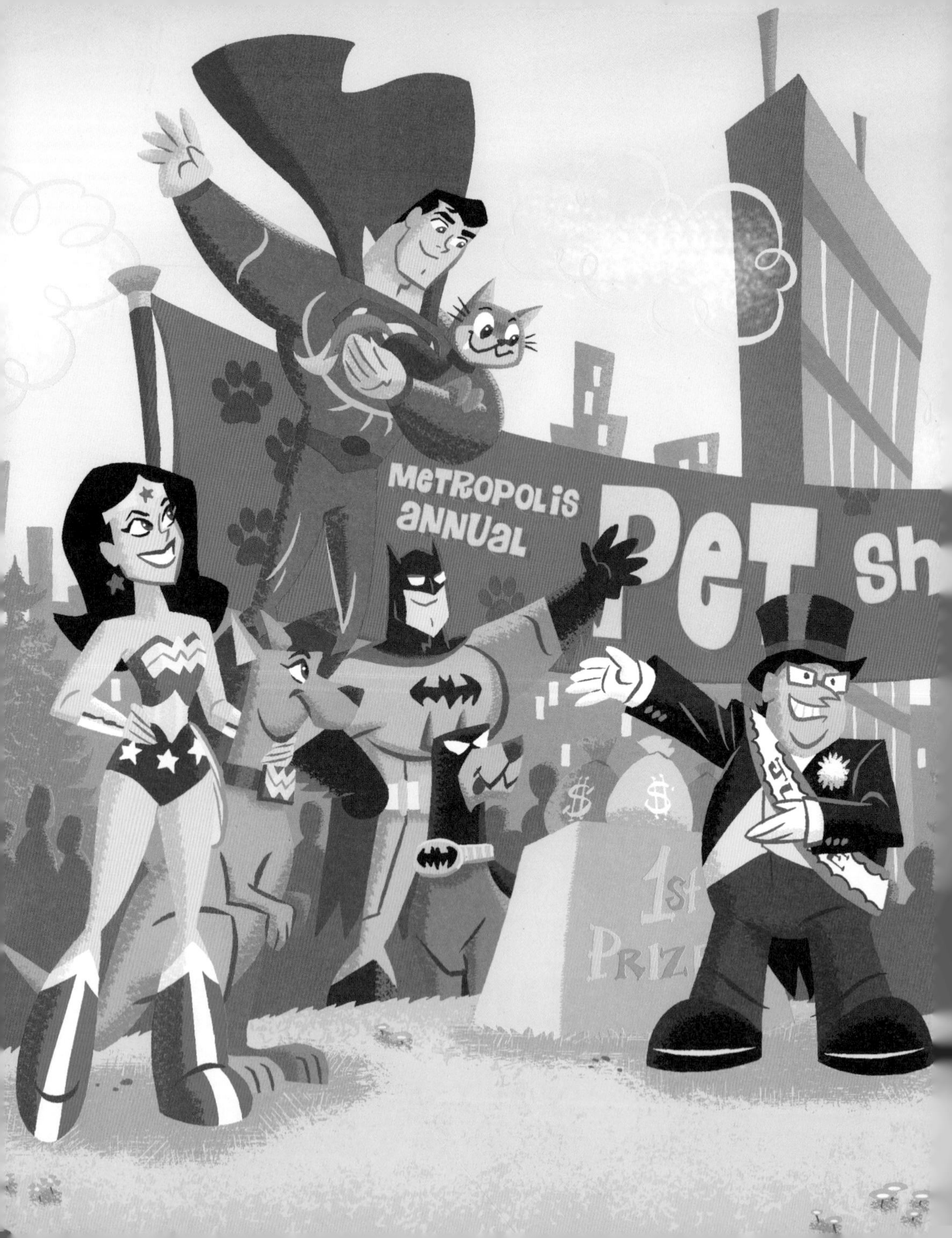
METROPOLIS ANNUAL
PET sh
1st
PRIZ

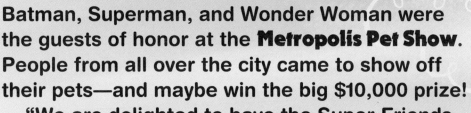

Batman, Superman, and Wonder Woman were the guests of honor at the **Metropolis Pet Show**. People from all over the city came to show off their pets—and maybe win the big $10,000 prize!

"We are delighted to have the Super Friends with us today," the judge told the roaring crowd. "And their amazing Super-Pets!"

Streaky the Super-Cat
flew through the air . . .

Wonder Woman's
kangaroo, **Jumpa**,
bounced and jumped . . .

. . . and **Ace** the **Bat-Hound** looked around, sniffing the air. He was always ready for trouble—just like Batman.

"Now let's see all these wonderful pets," the judge declared. The people and animals lined up. They began to parade past the judge and the Super Friends.

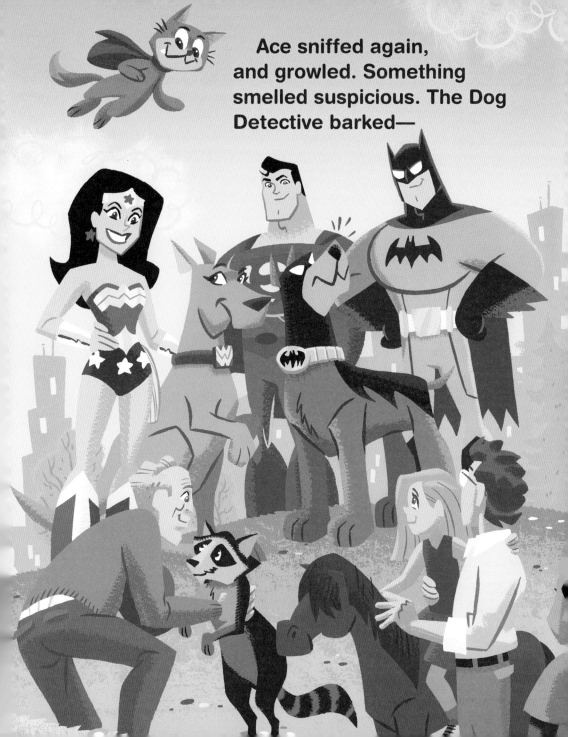

Ace sniffed again, and growled. Something smelled suspicious. The Dog Detective barked—

"The Joker!" Batman exclaimed as Ace pointed at one of the pet owners. "With his hyenas, **Crackers** and **Giggles**!"

"And Cheetah, with **Chauncey** the cat!" Wonder Woman said, spotting the feline villainess.

"Come out, Croc," Superman called.
"I see you—and **Anna Conda**, too."
"They must be here to steal the prize money," Wonder Woman said.

"I promise we're not up to any funny business," the Joker said. "We just want our pets to be in the show!"

Giggles and Crackers howled in agreement.

"There's no rule against super-villains being in the show," the judge declared. "I suggest we have a contest of Super-Pets!" The crowd cheered.

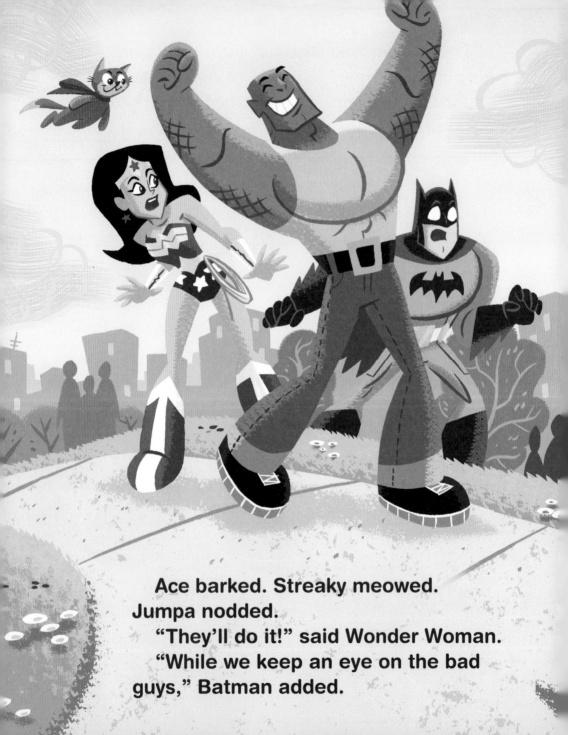

Ace barked. Streaky meowed.
Jumpa nodded.

"They'll do it!" said Wonder Woman.

"While we keep an eye on the bad
guys," Batman added.

The judge said the first contest would be a high jump.

"Hop to it," Wonder Woman told Jumpa. To everyone's surprise, Anna Conda coiled herself into a spring and bounced higher than Jumpa!

The second contest was an obstacle course. Ace dashed through it in record time. But Crackers and Giggles didn't even finish—they crashed into each other at the starting line!

"That's okay, boys. We can still laugh about it," the Joker said.

The final contest was a race between
Streaky and Chauncey. But as soon
as the cats started, Streaky saw
something. He couldn't believe his
super-vision—the judge was stealing
the prize money!

Ace barked, and all
the pets leapt into action!

Jumpa leaned back on her tail and used her powerful legs to launch Chauncey into the air.

Chauncey nimbly bounced off the lamppost and into the judge's chest. Ace and Crackers pulled Anna Conda tight like a rope, tripping the judge. He fell backward.

Giggles and Streaky made sure that the judge couldn't get away. Ace pulled away the judge's disguise, revealing—

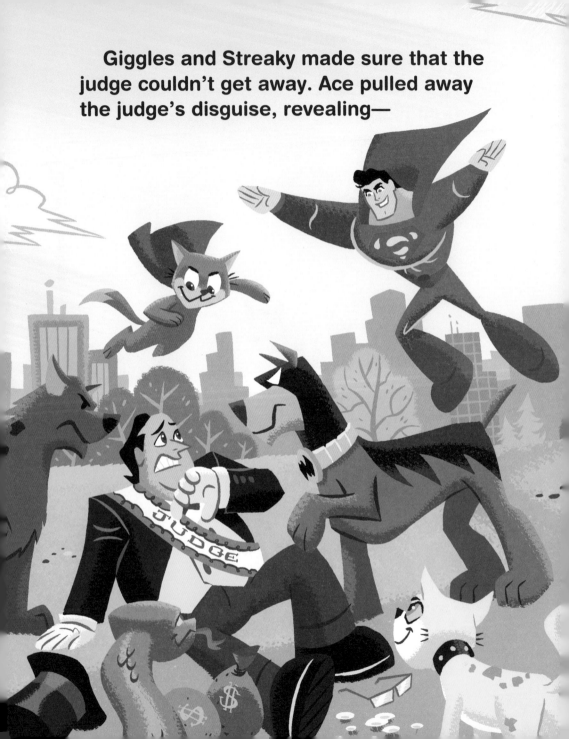

"The Penguin!" Cheetah snarled in surprise. "Only a villain as **fowl** as you would try to steal money from the Pet Show."

Batman turned the Penguin over to the guards while Superman put the prize money back in its rightful place.

"Today has been *grrrreat*," Croc rumbled, hugging Anna Conda.

"Having the love of a good pet makes us all winners," Wonder Woman said. The crowd cheered in agreement.

And with that, Ace, Streaky,
Jumpa, and the Super Friends
raced off to their next adventure!